READY, SET, SCREAM!

Adapted by Ximena Hastings

Ready-to-Read

Simon Spotlight
New York London Toronto Sydney New Delhi

SIMON SPOTLIGHT
An imprint of Simon & Schuster Children's Publishing Division
1230 Avenue of the Americas, New York, New York 10020
This Simon Spotlight edition July 2020

Manufactured in the United States of America 0620 LAK
10 9 8 7 6 5 4 3 2 1
ISBN 978-1-5344-6417-9 (hc)
ISBN 978-1-5344-6419-3 (pbk)
ISBN 978-1-5344-6418-6 (eBook)

Every hundred years,
the monsters at Hotel Transylvania
celebrate a spooky holiday . . .

It is called . . . Scream Day!

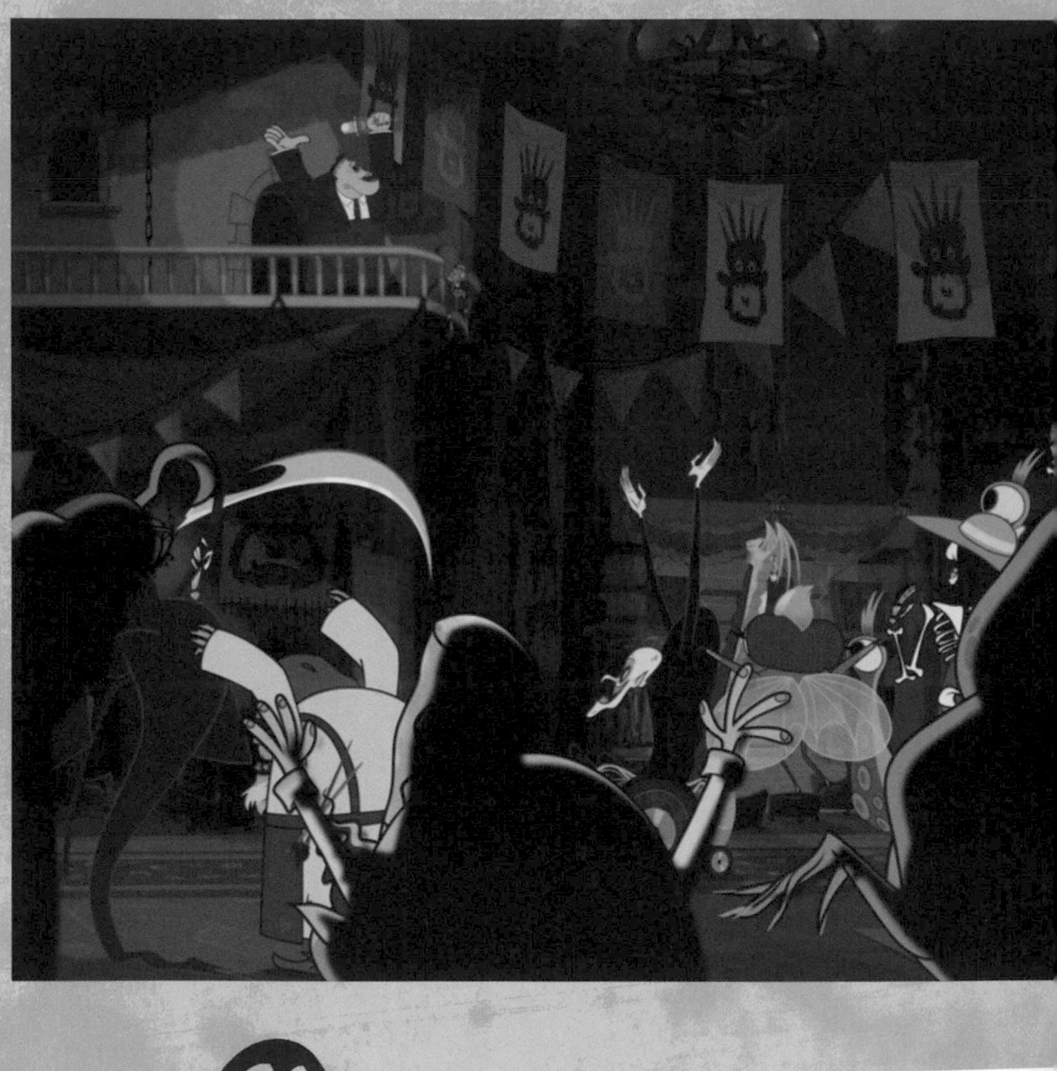

Monsters come from far and wide to scare each other. The monster who makes Larry the Leech scream the loudest wins a . . . *Screamie Award*!

“The highest scores are tracked on the Scare-O-Meter 2000!” the crowd was told.

This year Mavis was expected
to participate.
She opened her first Scream Day
card from her dad. Dracula wrote:
*Dear Mavis, just do your best,
which means—win!*

Mavis rolled her eyes.
“I want nothing to do with
this day. This is my dad’s deal,
not mine,” she said.

"Mavis, your dad is the greatest Scream Day champ of all time," Hank said. "Every hundred years your dad has won the Screamie. Now that he's away, this is the perfect chance for you to win!"

But Mavis does not care.
Her friends do, though.
They want to win the award!
They try out their biggest scares.
Wendy sneaks up on
Diane the Chicken!

Pedro burps so loud, he blows
the skeletons right off
some monsters.
Even Hank gets a few Screamie points
by accidentally tripping over
Larry and spooking him!

Everyone is having fun trying to earn their screams . . . everyone, except Aunt Lydia, of course.

All Aunt Lydia wants is for Mavis to carry on the Dracula family tradition and win. She demonstrates how it is done.

Mavis finally gave in.
"Fine! If everyone wants me to win the Screamie so bad, I will do it!" she shouted.

But since Aunt Lydia took the lead
with a rare “triple slay” scream,
the only way for Mavis to win was to
scare a *real human*!
“Done and done!” Mavis said.

Mavis turned into a bat
and flew out of the hotel.
"I am going to scare a human,
win the Screamie, and be the champion
for one hundred years!" she
announced.

Mavis approached the human's house
and saw Mrs. Cartwright standing
by the window.
Mavis was certain she could scare her.

Just then Mavis saw something that made *her* scream!

When Mavis got back to the hotel,
she was told she won because she had
screamed so loud!
Her friends were so proud of her,
they started calling her
"Mavis, Frightener of Humans!"

Mavis did not know how to tell her aunt Lydia or her friends the truth.

She knew it was *her* scream and not the *human* who let out the loudest scream of the night, but she did not want to let anyone down.

Aunt Lydia was so surprised Mavis won the Screamie, she wanted to see Mavis in monster-action!

“You can scare the human again with me by your side,” Aunt Lydia suggested.

"I would love to, Aunt Lydia, but it was a surprise . . . I don't think I could do it again," Mavis replied.

"I bet you could do it anyway,"
Hank said.
"You are so good!" Pedro agreed.
"Yeah! Do it! Do it!" Wendy cheered.

"Okay . . . ," Mavis agreed nervously.
"I'm right behind you, Aunt Lydia!"
While Aunt Lydia flew away to
find the humans, Mavis told
her friends the truth.

"I am the one who screamed tonight, *not* Mrs. Cartwright!" Mavis admitted. "What did you see?" Wendy asked.

"It is too horrible to tell," Mavis said. She screamed again, remembering the horror of it.

“Mavis, I said let’s go!”
Aunt Lydia called.
“Coming!” Mavis said.
They both flew out to the
Cartwrights’ home.
They peeked out from
behind a tree.

“Looks like no one is home.
I guess we should go back to the hotel,” Mavis suggested.
Aunt Lydia is not convinced.
She headed toward the house.

“Stop!” Mavis said, pulling Aunt Lydia down to the ground. “Once you see what is inside, you can never *un-see* it,” Mavis warned her.

“I knew it!” Aunt Lydia yelled.
“You didn’t scare anyone!”
She kept walking toward the window.

Mavis and Aunt Lydia looked inside the house and saw Mrs. Cartwright with her baby.
She was . . . changing a dirty diaper!

Aunt Lydia and Mavis let out the loudest scream in all of Scream Day history.

"We have a winner!" Frankenstein announced.